Little Wolf's
Book
of
Badness

WANTED

BIGBAD

HÜGE
REWARD

Little Wolf's
Book
of
Badness

Ian Whybrow
Illustrated by Tony Ross

Carolrhoda Books, Inc., Minneapolis

J
WHY

Carolrhoda Books, Inc., a Division of Lerner Publishing Group
241 First Avenue North, Minneapolis, MN 55401 U.S.A.

www.lernerbooks.com

Library of Congress Cataloging-in-Publication Data

Whybrow, Ian.
    Little Wolf's book of badness / Ian Whybrow ; illustrated by Tony Ross.
    p.   cm.
    Summary: Little Wolf has been behaving too courteously, so his parents
send him to his uncle's Big Bad Wolf school to learn to be a proper wolf.
ISBN 1-57505-410-8 (alk. paper)

[1. Wolves—Fiction. 2. Behavior—Fiction.
3. Uncles—Fiction.]
I. Ross, Tony, ill. II. Title.
PZ7.W6225Li 1999
[Fic]—dc21   99-30596

Manufactured in the United States of America
1 2 3 4 5 6 —BP—05 04 03 02 01 00

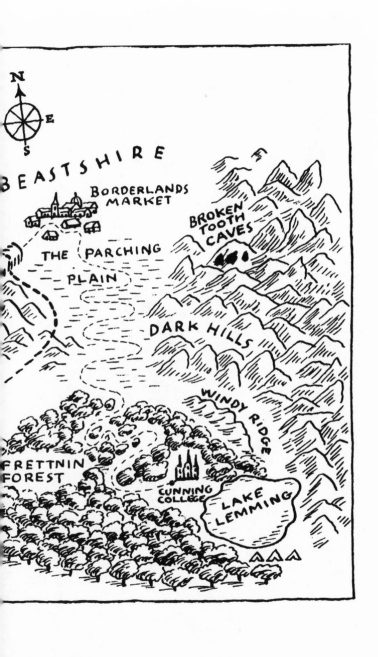

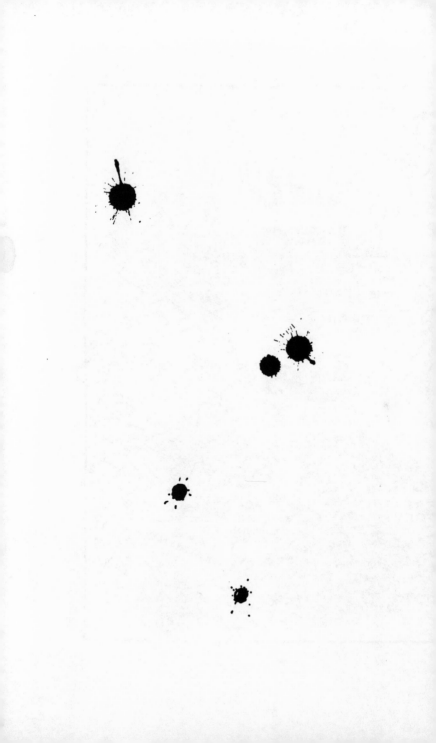

Little Wolf's
Book
of
Badness

Dear Mom and Dad,

Please please PLEEEEEZ let me come home. I have been walking and walking all day, and guess how far? Not even 10 miles, I bet. I have not even reached Lonesome Lake yet. You know I hate going on adventures. So why do I have to go hundreds of miles to Uncle Bigbad's school in the middle of a dark, damp forest?

You say you do not get on in life these days without a BAD badge. But I know lots of really bad wolves who never went to school. Ever. Like my cousin Yeller, for one. I know you want me to be wild and wicked like Dad, but why do I have to go so far away? Just what is so wonderful about Cunning College in Frettnin Forest? And what is so terrific about having Uncle Bigbad as a teacher? Is it all because Dad went to

Brutal Hall and they made him a hall monitor
and he got a silver BAD badge when he left? I
bet it is.

It is another four days' walk, maybe more,
to Frettnin Forest. Let me come back and learn
to be bad at home.

PLEE-EE-EEZ!!!

Your number 1 cub,

Little Wolf

P.S. Don't forget to say Hello, baby
bro to Smellybreff and tell him to
not touch any of my things.

Dear Mom and Dad,

I am a bit lost.

I think I have come to Lonesome Lake just where the River Rover runs up to it. I used Dad's map as a tablecloth for my picnic lunch. Now it is hard to tell if you have come to a river or a piece of bacon rind.

I have not heard from you to return home, so I must continue on this stupid, long journey, even though I might never find Uncle Bigbad. He never answers Dad's letters. Maybe Cunning College is closed, and he has moved from Frettnin Forest. Anyway, how will I know I have found him when I do?

BIGBAD

HUGE REWARD

I have the Wanted poster that you gave me, but it is years old. Maybe he has changed. What will he look like now? Too scary, I bet!

The sun fell in the water, and I did not like it. Then the moon came up, and now I can see my pen and paper, but I wish it was brighter. My tent is stupid. It falls down all the time, so I have curled up in my knapsack. Camping is my worst thing, and maps, too. I am frozz, I am hopeless.

Yours tiredoutly,

Little Wolf

Dear Mom and Dad,

I woke up this morning feeling tickly, with ants in my knapsack. They were small, but there were plenty of them, quite tasty for breakfast. Then I was more cheery. I started walking soon after the sun jumped out. It was hiding behind a hill.

3 hours later

I have stopped now for a rest and one of Mom's rabbit rolls. Yum yum—but only 25 left. Boo, shame. Shall probably starve... You know I am a hopeless hunter.

You just think I am a goody-goody, I bet. Is that why I have to go away for badness lessons? But I told you I only brushed my teeth last week for a joke. And combing my fur and going to bed early were just tricks to trick you! You ask my cousin Yeller. It was his idea. He

15

said, "Let's pretend being good." I just said OK. So I pretended. Then you were s'posed to say, "Oh no, Little Wolf has gone loony." Then I was s'posed to say, "Arr Harr, tricked you, I am a bad boy, really." But no, you would not listen. You did not understand. You said I must go to Cunning College, and I must live in Frettnin Forest until I get my BAD badge and learn Uncle Bigbad's 9 Rules of Badness.

I bet you won't make Smellybreff leave home when he is my age. You will just say, "Oh yes, my darling baby pet. You stay here safe with us and watch TV all you want." And what about Yeller? I 'spect you think he is a small, bad wolf, but no. You do not see him doing good things like I do. Like the kite he made for me to take with me, with yellow wolf eyes painted on it. And sometimes he says excuse me when he burps, too. I bet his mom and dad are nice and do not send him to school in a faraway forest.

Yours fedduply,

Little Wolf

Dear Mom and Dad,

Aah! The hunters got me in Lonesome Woods—urg.

Only kidding. I am all right, really. Had you worried though, huh?

Walked miles today and got to Spring Valley, but still have a long, long way to go. Have eaten most of Mom's rabbit rolls already. Boo, shame. I can smell your present for Uncle Bigbad—lots of yummy mice pies. Yes please, yum, chomp, chomp (not really).

I wonder if Uncle is as greedy as you said. I hope he is not ~~crool~~ cruel. I am only small. That reminds me. Tell my baby bro Smellybreff to not chew my teddy bear, or I will chew him back.

Dad's map is a little bit wrong, because there is no big, black monster between Lonesome Woods and Murky Mountains. I looked and looked, but there are only trees here. Off to Roaring River tomorrow.

Love from

Little Wolf

P.S. Oh dear. It was not a big, black monster on the map. It was a squashed ant. Sorry.

Dear Mom and Dad,

I am writing this under a bridge at a town called Roaring River. This makes six bridges I have crossed on my journey, and I'm still not even in Beastshire yet. I am sure it is much much farther to Frettnin Forest than Dad said.

Spent last night in a bus shelter. Quite warm and unscary, with my flashlight set to switch on and off. Mom always says yellow eyes are friends with the dark. True, but it is still nice to have a flashlight when you are a small loner.

Roaring River is too big—not a good place to wake up. There are so many human people here you would not believe. It is not safe for cubs.

Yours watchingly,

Little

Dear Mom and Dad,

Spent the day in Roaring River. I like the cars. They are nice and smelly and good growlers. And buses are best of all. They go FSSSHHH when they stop, and the people line up and get inside them. It is funny, just like Dad eating sausages.

This morning I wanted to try being a sausage. So I got in a line behind a large woman at the bus stop. Then guess what! She hit me with her shopping bag just for wearing a fur coat. She said, "Take that for animal rights."

I said, "Stop! I am an animal!" She said, "What sort?" So I told her, and she ran off screaming. Har, har.

Her shopping was quite tasty, except some white powdery stuff in a box. It made my tongue all bubbly...

Yours spittily,

Little Wolf

Dear Mom and Dad,

I was glad to leave Roaring River. Feel a bit better after a good gargle in a stream, and all the nasty foam spit out.

Got to Crowfeet Crossroads by noon. Nice houses here, but not as nice as our smelly cave. Did not see any people, only a mailbox to mail this.

I had a think today. Do you know what? Everybody else thinks I am bad, even if you think I am a goodie-4-paws. Remember when Mom was asleep that time and I snipped off her whiskers with the claw clippers? And

what about when I glued Smellybreff's tail to his high chair? So whyo Y do I have to make this stupid, long journey?

Just now I thought I heard Yeller calling me. It was only a train howling in the valley. I am going now up the steep and wiggly path through the Murky Mountains. It looks VERY dangerous. Hope you are satisfied.

Farewell from

L. Wolf

Dear M and D,

I had some big shocks today.

You did not say how cold it gets up in the mountains. You have to climb up and up above Crowfeet Crossroads. Sometimes you are up so high that nothing grows, not even trees. And the ice makes your feet slip. Two times I nearly skidded right over the edge of the path. It was terrible. When I peeped over, the houses down below looked as small as sparrows' nests.

Then I got lost. I followed one thin path. It just went around and around and came back where I started. So I wrote TRICK PATH

in big letters on a rock for the next traveler.
And off I went fedduply.

Just before dark I found the edge of
Murkshire. I felt sleepy and wanted to lie
down. My breath was white clouds. Then I saw
a deep, dark tunnel going into a mountain wall
and a sign above the entrance. It said:

My fur started jumping up all along my back. But I did not want to stay in the open and freeze. So I took a big breath and went in, running, running. I shouted, "Can't scare me. Yellow eyes are friends with the dark!" Then guess what! My words shouted back—only louder and growlier! I ran and ran with my puff hot in my throat. I had just enough puff to get to the end. It was the best feeling ever to be in the open, looking at the moon shining down. It was shining on the village of Borderlands Market.

And that was how I got here.
Just.

Can't keep awake. More tomorrow.

L.

Dear Mom and Dad,

Guess who woke me up
this morning? I will give
you a clue. He has sharp
eyes, a pointy face, red
bristly fur, and a smell
like pepper.

I was all curled up under a small cart near a
streetlight in the market square—*zzzz*—fast
asleep. All of a suddenly, I felt hot breath in my
ear and heard this voice saying, "My boy!" I
jumped up and banged my head. I tried to run,
but strong paws held me down, and then I
yelled, "Ooo-er, a fox!"

The fox said, "Mister Twister is my name. You are camping under my stall." I said, "Whoops, sorry, Mister Twister." He said, "Do not worry yourself, my boy. There will be no charge. For now. But then, something tells me you are a bright young laddie who is eager to assist me with my work today."

I did not know how to say no to him. More later.

Yours stuckly,

Little

Dear Mom and Dad,

Yesterday I did work at the market for Mister Twister. He sells dizgizzes (cannot spell it). My job was putting on phony beards, masks, sheep's clothing, etc., and walking up and down saying, "Hey, guess what I am?" It was fun dressing up, and lots of people stopped to buy things.

A small mouse came up to me and said, "I am lonely. Can you sell me something to help me make friends?" I said, "Yes, I can. Here are some tie-on wings. Wear these and stand on your head. Then lots of bats will come and play with

you." And guess what? He bought 2 pairs!

And my best thing was finding something for a weasel to wear to a fancy dress ball. I sold him half a coconut and told him to shave all his fur off. Then he could go as a tortoise! He was so pleased he said I could keep the change.

I like being a market worker.

Yours richly,

Little

Dear Mom and Dad,

Mister Twister said I was a good worker and would I stay? I wanted to, but I told him I had to go to Cunning College and study for my BAD badge. "You amaze me!" he said, and his sharp eyes went wide, and his red fur went even more bristly. "Do you mean to tell me that you are going to Cunning College in Frettnin Forest?"

I said, "Yes, do you know it?"

He said, "My boy, I was a teacher in that school many a full moon ago! Your uncle and I used to be partners! Can you really be the nephew of that nasty, mean, bad, horrid crook?"

I said a proud "Yes."

The fox told me more. He and Uncle Bigbad met ages ago in Broken Tooth Caves when they were both hiding from the police. Uncle had the idea to stay out of sight in Frettnin Forest and start a school for bad beasts. He promised Mister Twister that if he worked hard, teaching the naughty pupils everything he knew, he would soon be rich.

Mister Twister said, "My boy, it was dreadful. The pupils never gave me a moment's peace! They were awfully sly and squirmy, all those little skunks and weasels and rattlesnakes and cubs! How they got on my nerves, those spoiled little brutes! And what a fuss their horrid parents made, always wanting to know when their ghastly offspring would be getting their BAD badges! They quite wore me out. But when I asked your uncle for some money, just enough to allow me to take a short jaunt, he threatened to eat me!"

I said, "What did he say?"

Mister Twister said, "He told me to get out, and he said that if I ever put a paw in his school again, he would boil my bones and serve me up as soup."

I said, "Ooo-er!"

The fox said, "So you see, your uncle is a miser and a cheat. He has bags of money hidden away, but he will not part with a penny of it. You would be unwise, my boy, to leave Borderlands Market. What is more, Frettnin Forest is a SHOCKING place—dismal, dark, and lonely. Your Uncle Bigbad is dangerous. He has a terrible temper. In short, he is Mister Mean. My strong advice to you, my boy, is STAY AWAY FROM CUNNING COLLEGE!"

I said, "Yikes, you have a point!"

Yours having a good think,

L.W.

Dear Mom and Dad,

I am a bit confused and bothered. Mister Twister wants me to stay with him forever and be his dresser-upper. Sometimes I think, Oh yes, nice idea, because one day I could have a stall of my own. Next thing I think, Yes, but what about learning the 9 Rules of Badness? If I do not, how will I get a BAD badge and keep up the good name of Wolf?

But Mister Twister has got me worried about Uncle. I mean, about boiling him up as soup. If Uncle is going to make soup out of his large friend, what will he make out of a small nephew he has never met? Will I be his special pupil, or just a sausage in a sandwich?

Yours nervously,

Little

The Parching Plain
Day 9

Dear Mom and Dad,

I have decided. I am going on. I think I like adventures now. (A little bit, anyway.) Tell Smells and Yeller for me. It will be a good shock for them.

I slipped away from Borderlands Market very early before Mister Twister came and talked softly to me. I did not trust his voice. I still have the bonnet he gave me for dressing up as an old lady. It might come in handy.

Borderlands Market and the mountains are far behind me now. Today was my longest walk ever. One good thing—the land was flat. But no shade for miles and miles. On the map it is called The Parching Plain, and now I know why. The track was dusty and the sun was hot. I hoped to find a stream to splash my tongue in, but no luck. I wished I had brought a snowball from the mountains to lick.

In the afternoon some big birds came, big as planes. They glided around and around. The slower I walked, the lower the birds flew. About 4 o'clock one came close enough to show his hooked beak and claws.

Then I remembered Yeller's present, my kite with the yellow wolf eyes painted on it. I had to stop to get it out of my knapsack and put it together. Now the birds came so low I could see their shadows flick on the stones near me. I howled to make them stay back, and then I was ready.

I tugged the string, and the kite FLEW up. I flipped and flapped it right in their ugly faces. You should have seen them scatter! They were like tadpoles in a pond when you plop in a pebble!

Don't forget to tell Yeller. I kept his kite flying across The Parching Plain and not one bird bothered me again.

I am mailing this just on the edge of Frettnin Forest. I have not gone in yet, but tomorrow I will have to. Ooo-er. It looks darker in there than the Borderlands Tunnel.

Good thing I can whistle, huh?

Yours chinupply,

Little W.

Dear Mom and Dad,

I have arrived. It took me all day with the paths so overgrown. But I have found Uncle's school at last. The fox was right. This IS the shockingest, dismalest, darkest part of the forest.

Much too late to ring the doorbell. If I wake up Uncle now, he is sure to eat me.

I have tried putting up my tent, but it's no good. So I have made a small den in a bush in the college garden—OK, but a little bit prickly.

Oh no, now it is drizzling here! Sorry about the smudges. I wish I was curled up under my nice, dry rock at home.

Talk about spooky. So overgrown, with eyes and croaks and squeaks everywhere! Good thing I have my flashlight. I am holding it in my mouth to see what I am writing. Also, I can point it and light up a sign by the door of the schoolhouse from here. It says:

Gosh—sorry about that. Something went WOO—made me jump. This is SO scary, it stands your fur up.

Not sure when I will find a mailbox, but I just want to say something. OK, I did teach my little brother "Eensy Weensy Spider," and "The Wheels on the Bus," with actions, I admit that. But those were just tricks, honest. You know I am not really nice and polite. I do not usually brush my teeth, or my fur either. You ask Yeller. I just hope Uncle isn't too cruel. I do not want to get boiled.

This could be my last letter.

Ever.

And it will be all your fault.

Yours damply,

Master L. Wolf

P.S. Smellybreff can have my ted, but I promised Yeller my box of tricks.

Dear Mom and Dad,

Guess what, not dead yet!

Woke up this morning so damp and frozz, I thought, okay, be brave. Better to be boiled than to die frozz. So I went *ding ding* on the doorbell.

Next thing, *boom boom!* Big feet came down the hall, and lots of huff and puff. The door went *eeeeee-aaaaah,* and there was Uncle Bigbad, all tall and thin and horrible. He is not like in the Wanted poster. His eyebrows are furry like caterpillars, and they join in the middle. He is very fierce, and he has great big red eyes, and big, long yellow teeth, and great big, long streams of dribble dribbling down. He reminds me a little bit of Dad, but hungrier. And he wears a great big gold BAD badge on his chest.

So I took a big breath to get steady, but my voice went wobbly. "H-h-h-hello Uncle Badbiggy, I am your n-nephew L-little Wolf. M-mom and Dad sent me so you can t-teach me the 9 R-rules of B-badness."

He snarled his great big, horrible snarl, and he said in his great big, horrible voice, "GRRRR! BEGONE, VILE BALL OF FLUFF! FLY AND FLEE, OR I SHALL FETCH THE VACUUM CLEANER AND SUCTION YOU UP OFF MY FRONT STEP!"

I said, "B-b-but I am your nephew, L-little W-wolf. Didn't you get Dad's l-l-letters?"

He said, "GRRRR, I HAVE

CEASED TO RECEIVE LETTERS."

I said, "Why?"

He said, "BECAUSE THE MAILMEN WILL NOT DELIVER. JUST BECAUSE I DEVOURED 1 OR 2 OF THEM! IT IS NOT FAIR. I AM ALWAYS STARVING THESE DAYS! IN FACT, SPEAKING OF FOOD, STAND STILL A MINUTE WHILE I PUT SOME SALT AND PEPPER ON YOU!"

I said, "Wait, Uncle, do not devour me. Try some rabbit rolls! I think I have 2 left. They are a little stale, sorry, but tastier than me."

He said, "GRRRR, GIVE THEM TO ME, SWIFTLY, SWIFTLY!" Then he grabbed them and banged the door in my face—*bang!*

Gulp. I am coming home.

Yours trembly,
Litfly

Frettnin Forest
Day 12

Dear Mom and Dad,

I started going back along the
forest path, running, running. I felt
awful—no BAD badge, no lessons,
nothing. Then I thought, Oh no, the
shame. What will Mom and Dad say if
I go home now? Oh boo, now I will
have to camp out forever, which is my
worst thing.

Then, *ding!* I had an idea—
Mom's mice pies that she made
for Uncle's present! I hid half the
pies in a hollow tree. Then I turned
around, and I went *creep creep* to
the college again. The mailbox was
too small, so I went around the back
and climbed onto the roof. I got
1 mice pie and tied it to a long
string off my kite. (Good old Yeller!)
Then I let it down the chimney.

Next thing, I heard Uncle say,

"SNIFF SNUFF SNY!

I SMELL PIE!"

And then Uncle's great big, long tongue went SLIP SLAP. You could hear him going mad looking for pies, crashing the furniture all around. So I jiggled the string. All of a suddenly, *WOOOOOF*—gone! No more mice pie.

Next I let down a little note. It said:

And guess what?

I am IN.

Your brainy boy,

L. Wolf, ESQ.

Dear Mom and Dad,

What a shock when I first went inside! Cunning College was empty except for Uncle, and dust and cobwebs everywhere. Not one pupil was left in the classroom. I said to Uncle, "Where are all the pupils?"

He said, "DEPARTED, SCATTERED! I AM SO *FRIGHTFULLY* FRIGHTENING, THEY ALL FLED AND FLEW AWAY! NOW GIVE ME MORE PIES! GRRRR! SWIFTLY, SWIFTLY!"

What could I do? I gave him one, and down it went—GULP. Then he said, "MORE PIES, MORE! GRRRR! SWIFTLY! SWIFTLY!"

So I said, "If I give you 1 more mice pie, will you be my teacher?"

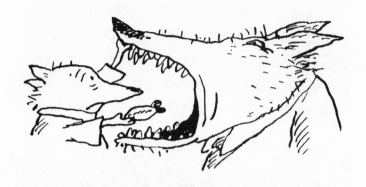

He did not listen. He only swallowed the pie—GULP. Then he said,

"MORE, MORE! I MUST HAVE MORE! MORE MICE PIES, OR I'LL EAT *YOU!*"

I said, "But Uncle!"

He said, "BUT WHAT?!" And he HUFFED and he PUFFED, and he PUFFED and he HUFFED.

I thought, Oh no, he will kill me dead. But I got my braveness up. I said, "There are lots more pies hidden in the forest! You can have them, but—teaching first, pies after."

And guess what! He went all nice. He said, "OH MY DEAR, SPLENDID, HANSUM NEPHEW, PLEASE LET ME TEACH YOU BAGS OF BADNESS."

He says we start lessons tomorrow. And tonight I am sleeping in the *dorm!*

Yours proudly,

Little

Day 14

Dear Mom and Dad,

Slept in the dorm last night. It was nice, but not as cozy and smelly as home. Boo, shame. I wished some other pupils were there. Never mind, because guess what! I found a big mirror and had a pillow fight with myself!

I got up early and did *grrrrs* for practice. I have a little bit of a sore throat now, but I think I am quite scary. Then I sharpened my pencils and color crayons and pointed them all the same way so I was ready for class.

My first lesson that I learned today was this: Small wolves clean up, and big wolves sit down and watch TV.

Kind of sad, huh? I thought we would be doing badness, but no.

Uncle got huffy and puffy and said all his pupils must clean the blackboard, swat the flies, polish the desks, shoo the spiders, and scrub the floor, windows, and bathrooms.

So I did. It took me a long time—nearly till dark. Uncle said, "GRRRR, WHY ARE YOU SO SLOW, FURBALL?"

I said, "I am not slow, but everything is filthy dirty."

That was the wrong answer. Uncle sent me to bed and ate my supper.

Yours hohummly,

Litty

Day 15

Dear Mom and Dad,

No cleaning today, hooray! And guess what? I have learned 2 Rules of Badness already!

I found a clean notebook in one of the desks, and I wrote in it:

Uncle came into the classroom. He was shining up his big gold BAD badge with his sleeve. I said, "Hum, nice! When will I get my badge?"

Uncle was nasty. He said, "NOT UNTIL YOU KNOW THE 9 RULES OF BADNESS, AND THAT WILL TAKE YOU YEARS AND YEARS, BECAUSE YOU ARE NOT CRAFTY ENOUGH TO FIND THEM OUT SWIFTLY."

I said, "Maybe not, but I am still going to try my hardest."

Uncle said, "VERY WELL, MY CLUELESS CUB. LET US START WITH A STORY THAT MIGHT HELP YOU OUT. 2 RULES OF BADNESS ARE HIDDEN IN IT, BUT YOU ARE MUCH TOO SMALL AND HOPELESS TO FIND THEM!"

I said, "Never mind, tell me the story anyway."

So Uncle smiled his big, horrible smile, and he began.

"ONCE UPON A TIME, THERE WERE 3 LITTLE PIGGIES, AND THEY GOT ON MY NERVES SINGING THAT THEY WERE NOT AFRAID OF THE BIGBAD WOLF. AND THEY KEPT GOING '*HA-HA-HA-HA-HA*' ALL THE

TIME. SO I HUFFED AND I PUFFED, AND I BLEW THEIR HOUSES DOWN AND ATE THEM."

I made a joke. I said, "Gosh, Uncle, imagine eating their houses! Were the bricks tasty?"

Uncle said, "SILENCE, SPECK! THAT IS NOT FUNNY! GRRRR! I ONCE HAD A BLASTED DREADFUL ACCIDENT WITH A BRICK HOUSE! I NEARLY BLEW MY HEAD OFF TRYING TO HUFF IT DOWN! SO, YOU BLINKING BLUNKER, KEEP QUIET ABOUT BRICK HOUSES!"

I said, "Well now, I think I can make a guess. I know what Rules 1 and 2 are, Uncle! The answer is:

RULE 1. HUFF AND PUFF A LOT.

RULE 2. SAY LOTS OF RUDE WORDS."

Uncle got very angry. He said, "GRRRR! HOW DO YOU KNOW THAT? YOU MUST HAVE CHEATED! SOMEBODY TOLD YOU THOSE RULES!"

I said, "Nobody told me! I guessed!" And I wrote Rules 1 and 2 in my Book of Badness.

He went, "GRRRR!" and took a bite out of the sink.

Love from

Littly

Day 16

Dear Mom and Dad,

My 3rd day at Cunning College, and Uncle has stopped my lessons. He said there was nothing in the pantry and I must go for food. I said, "Do you mean go to the store? The stores are miles away."

He said, "SILENCE, MOANER! I HAVE NO MONEY, THEREFORE YOU WILL HAVE TO HUNT FOR OUR LUNCH IN FRETTNIN FOREST. BRING ME BACK A SQUIRREL BURGER, SWIFTLY, SWIFTLY!"

I thought, funny—didn't that fox say Uncle had bags of money hidden somewhere?

Oh dear. I spent ages trying to catch squirrels, but I am hopeless at climbing trees. All I got were just some ants and earwigs for crunchy snacks.

Uncle was mad for a bit when I got back. He growled and kicked the stuffing out of the sofa. (He was quite scary, but no more than Dad.) Then he ate the crunchy snacks and went to

bed. He says it is the new moon tomorrow, therefore he must get his strength up.

He would not even stop to check my work in my Book of Badness, so not much badgework yet. But do not fret and frown. I will soon be the baddest boy in the pack.

Yours youbettly,

L.

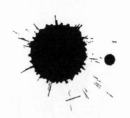

Day 17

Dear M and D,

Boring, boring, boring. The most interesting thing today was it rained. Here is a poem I wrote, called BORING SNORING:

> It's raining, it's boring
> Uncle Bigbad is snoring
> He howls all night
> And he looks such a sight
> And he never gets up when you call him.

Little

This is me trying to wake him up:

New moon
Day 18

Dear Mom and Dad,

I feel like running away. It is awful here. No other cubs to play with, nothing to do, nothing to eat, and you do not even get letters because of Uncle eating the mailmen. I am starting to wonder if he is as brainy as he keeps saying he is. I have not learned a thing except huffing and puffing, and no new rude words either. I could stand it if Yeller was here to talk to, or even Smellybreff. I am a very lone wolf.

I have not seen much of Uncle since I took him his breakfast in bed. I said to him, "Here is your nice breakfast. Now can you teach me the 3rd Rule of Badness?"

He said, "DO NOT DISTURB! I MUST SLEEP ALL DAY AND STAY AWAKE ALL NIGHT."

I said, "Doing what?"

He said, "BEING A TERROR!" And then he
said, "FLY AND FLEE, SMALL FLUFFBALL.
GO OUTSIDE AND DO SOME QUIET
HUFFING PRACTICE."

I did what he said. I huffed and puffed in
the garden, but it made me dizzy just blowing
dandelions

Yours fedduply,

Little

Day 19

Dear Mom and Dad,

It is midnight and I cannot sleep. Uncle is on the roof, howling and howling at the moon. He goes on and on. He is not being a terror, just a pain.

I cannot stand it.

Please let me come home and I promise *promise* I will never read another book. I will stick crayons up my nose more often, and I will be rotten to Smellybreff all the time. I will be a real noosunce newsens ~~pain. Only don't make~~ me stay in this blunking blasted silly college. (See, I can say lots of rude words now. Can't you just be proud of that?) I cannot bear another night of Uncle's howling.

Yours ~~despritly~~ desperately,

Litfly

Day 20

Dear Mom and Dad,

Guess what? We had a visitor today, thrill thrill. It was a tall man with a berry on his head and a whistle on a string. I thought, yippee, somebody to try my *grrrrs* on. I opened the door *(eeeeee-arrrrrr)* and did my best *grrrr.*

He patted me on the head and said, "So sorry to bother you, sonny jim, but we are camping nearby. Could you possibly do something to fix the burglar alarm that kept going off on your roof last night? My poor cubs never slept a wink."

I said, "Fly and flee, immediate-lee!" But he did not seem to notice. He just saluted and said, "Thank you very much, sonny jim. Have a nice day."

He did not fool me with that story about cubs. No way is he a wolf. I wonder what trick he is up to.

I cannot ask Uncle—he is asleep again. Oh well. Must go and look for something to pounce on—I am starving.

Yours peckishly,

Littly

Day 20
Nighttime

Dear Mom and Dad,

Guess what! Just when I thought, Oh no, I will never learn any more Rules of Badness, I found out Number 3!

This is what happened 1ˢᵗ thing today. Uncle was up on the roof. I was having a good sniff around the kitchen looking for a snack. And do you know what? I found *lots* of food. There were ratflakes, and there was some dried vole and even half a moosecake! They were hidden in the back of a cupboard, and Uncle said there was no food in the house! The fox was right— he is a miser!

It made me stop and wonder. Perhaps Uncle has some hidden treasure somewhere after all!

I did not have time to search, because all of a suddenly, Uncle came down off the roof. Such a bad mood! He told me it was a waste of time howling, because the moon cheats. He said, "IT COMES NEARER AND NEARER, BUT JUST WHEN YOU HAVE HOWLED YOUR HEAD OFF AND YOU THINK IT IS CLOSE ENOUGH FOR YOU TO TAKE A NICE BIG CHEESY BITE OUT OF IT, IT BACKS AWAY!"

Then he crawled into bed all grumbly.

Thus and therefore, Uncle was fibbing! He was not trying to be a terror, just trying to get a free snack! What a greedy-guts!

So guess what? I do not think Uncle always tells the truth. And that is how I found out Rule 3. I wrote it down in my Book of Badness.

RULE 3. FIB YOUR HEAD OFF.

Yours sherlockholmesly,

Me

Day 21

Dear Mom and Dad,

A little tired today. I could not sleep because of thinking about the man with the whistle. Do you remember, he came to complain about Uncle being a burglar alarm? I have not told Uncle about him yet, because I have an idea. I am going to play a trick on that man, and then Uncle will most likely think, AHA! THAT IS A BLUNKING BLASTED GOOD TRICK, SO NOW I MUST TEACH THAT CRAFTY NEPHEW OF MINE LOTS MORE BADNESS.

My best idea so far is to stuff something up the man's whistle. Crafty, hm? But I am still trying to think of something even badder than that. See? I am trying my hardest to be like Uncle, so you can be proud of me.

I looked all over the forest to find the camp where the man said he keeps his cubs, but no luck yet. Still, I found a cottage not far from here. A girl lives there. I watched her all morning to see if she would be fun to play with, but not really. She is too busy dressing up in red riding hoods and taking picnics to her granny, etc. Boo, shame. I am quite surprised Uncle has not eaten her yet. But maybe he has noticed that her dad is a woodcutter with large muscles and a big, sharp axe.

My best news is, the girl took her dad a picnic, and guess what? She dropped 2 chicken legs out of her basket—yum yum!

I am saving them (big secret).

Your crafty

Little Wolf

Day 22

Dear Mom and Dad,

I gave Uncle one of the chicken legs I found, and that made him be in a really good mood. So I said to him, "I know where there are lots more."

Then I got my book out and I said, "Uncle, I have written down 3 rules in my Book of Badness. Can you teach me Number 4?"

He said, "PERHAPS, BUT HOW MANY MORE OF THOSE DELICIOUS CHICKEN LEGS CAN I HAVE?"

I said, "One now, Uncle, lots more later." (Only one really, but I was thinking of Rule 3— fib your head off.)

He said, "I ADORE CHICKEN LEGS, SO I WILL TELL YOU 2 RULES!"

I copied them carefully in my Book of Badness, like this:

RULE 4. IF IT SQUEAKS, EAT IT.
RULE 5. BLOW EVERYBODY DOWN.

This is easy cheesy!! Soon I will know all 9 Rules of Badness.

petit wolf (french)

Day 23

Dear Mom and Dad,

I keep after Uncle to teach me more Rules of Badness but he has gotten very snappish. He just says "HUFFING AND PUFFING" all the time, and I know that one. Also, he has moved the food in the kitchen to a new hiding place. I think he thinks I have been nibbling. (I ask you, would I? Hem, hem.)

Your puzzled

Littly

Day 24

Dear Mom and Dad,

Got another rule, hooray! It is:

RULE 6. DO YOUR DIRTIEST EVERY DAY.

Uncle has a big mirror in his room, all nice and dusty. He spent 4 hours yesterday gazing at himself, and he must have just scribbled it in the dust without noticing. (He loves himself so much!)

Quick as a chick, I put it down in my Book of Badness. Then I decided to go exploring and see if I could find anybody to do my dirtiest on. I went through Frettnin Forest and right over Dark Hills, looking for the man with the whistle and his cubs. And guess what? I found their camp down by Lake Lemming!

Sad to say, I could not think of a good trick to trick them. But I did do a trick on a beetle today. I said, "Hello, sonny, would you like to play a game?"

So he said, "OK, why not?" So I said, "Go on then, say, "What is the time, Mister Wolf?"'

So he said, "Why?" So I said, "You will see in a minute." So he said, "OK. What is the time, Mister Wolf?" and I said, "DINNERTIME, har, har!"

He was quite tasty.

Wait till Uncle hears that. He will make me a hall monitor, I bet!

Your best cub (tell that to Smellybreff—he will go mad, har, har),

Little

Day 25, I think
(just my luck if it is wensdie—
I cannot spell it!)

Dear Mom and Dad,

I told Uncle about tricking that beetle yesterday. He did not make me hall monitor. He got all jealous instead. He said, "GRRRRUBBISH, THAT IS NOT WICKED. THAT IS A GOODY-GOODY TRICK!"

Being kind of upset, I went out for a wander in the forest, and guess what? I bumped into the man with the whistle! He said, "Hello, sonny jim. I am the leader of a pack of Cub Scouts. We are camping down by Lake Lemming. Tomorrow we plan to have a barbecue. We hope you can join us. Here is an invitation." I snatched the invitation and said

CUB SCOUT
BARBECUE
7 o'clock
by LAKE
LEMMING

74

my scariest GRRRRAAH, but he said, "Oh dear, have you got a sore throat, sonny jim? Have a cough drop. Must dash now."

I ran back and told Uncle. He said, "A CUB SCOUT BARBECUE? YUM YUM, I LOVE CUB SCOUTS. DELICIOUS!"

I said, "Uncle, I think the pack leader wants us to go and eat his hot dogs, not his Cub Scouts."

But Uncle would not listen. He said, "I KNOW THEIR MOTTO. IT IS 'BE PREPARED.' THUS AND THEREFORE, I SHALL PREPARE SOME FOR THE OVEN AND THE REST FOR THE POT. NONE FOR YOU THOUGH, GRRRR."

Boo, shame. Uncle is too good at doing his dirtiest.

Yours upsettly,

Little

Day 26

Dear Mom and Dad,

Had an outdoor lesson today, learned Rule 7, and Uncle bit me.

At 1st Uncle was in a good mood, because he was plotting. He decided to catch the Cub Scouts by a trick called charming. (Have you heard of it? Me neither.) Anyway, Uncle showed me how you do charming on a mole.

We went to this field all covered in mole hills. I said, "What are we doing here, Uncle?"

He said, "I AM SHOWING YOU CHARMING. SO SILENCE, FLUFFBALL. OBSERVE AND LEARN FROM THE MASTER."

I watched and took notes. First he lay flat on his tummy. Then he smiled a big, horrible smile. Then he shouted down the mole hole, "GRRRR! LISTEN, MOLEY! COME OUT OR I WILL BASH YOUR HILLS IN!!!" And lastly, he took a running jump and *skwish!* He skwished the mole hill with his great big, horrible feet. I made notes in my Book of Badness like this:

How to do Charming:
 big smile,
 running jump,
 skwish hills.

I added:

Say horrible, growly things about bashing.

There were lots and lots of hills, and Uncle took ages jumping on them. And do you know what? We never even saw the mole.

He was hiding underground.

I said to Uncle, "I think charming is silly."
That is when he went mad and bot my bittom.
(Other way around, sorry.)

He said, "WAIT TILL YOU SEE ME
CHARMING THOSE CUB SCOUTS
TOMORROW!"

Yours sorebottomly,

Little

(nice pic of a mole, hm?)

CUNNING COLLEGE FOR BRUTE BEASTS

Day 27

Dear Mom and Dad,

What a flop! Uncle is in bed with a headache, and he did not catch one Cub Scout to eat, not even a hot dog. I will tell you about it.

Uncle sat and cooled his sore feet in a bath in front of the fire all morning. Suddenly he said, "AH, NOW I AM READY FOR SOME PROPER CHARMING." He drank his bathwater, burped, and dried his feet on the curtains. Then off we went to Windy Ridge. It was just before the sun hid.

It was frozz up on the ridge—it made your teeth ache. Uncle said we had to smile a big smile and stand in the north wind till it got stuck. It took ages. Then we had to kerlump through the forest in the dark and take our smiles to Lakeside Meadow.

79

Talk about hard—finding it in the dark—
and we were glad for the warm campfire. Uncle
stood frozz in the firelight looking all horrible,
like he had his tail
caught in a gate.

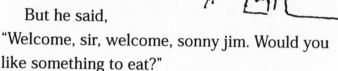

The pack leader
came up to us. I
thought, Oh no, trouble.

But he said,
"Welcome, sir, welcome, sonny jim. Would you
like something to eat?"

I was going to say I would have a nice warm
hot dog, but Uncle smiled his stuck-on smile
and said, "GRRRR! YESSS! GIVE ME YOUR
CUB SCOUTS, OR I'LL HUFF, AND I'LL PUFF,
AND I'LL BLOW YOUR TENTS DOWN!"

The pack leader shouted, "Quick, boys,
emergency!" He blew his whistle, and *bing!* All
the Cub Scouts jumped into their tents and
zipped up.

Uncle huffed and puffed his hardest.
Nothing happened. The tents dented a little bit,

but they stayed standing up. Uncle's cheeks went out like balloons, and he got redder and redder and redder. Then all of a suddenly, he twizzled around six times and fell on his nose.

I have written down Rule 7 in my Book of Badness. This is it:

RULE 7. DO CHARMING (SNEAKY SMILES).

I think Rule 7 is silly. I had to drag Uncle all the way home by his tail.

Yours tiredoutly,

Little

Day 28

Dear Mom and Dad,

Uncle has still got a bad head-and-tailache. He says he is dying (hem, hem) and will not get out of bed. I gave him the bonnet I took from Mister Twister at Borderlands Market. I said, "Here, this will keep your head warm." He put it on, then he told me to depart—swiftly, swiftly—so I went exploring in the forest.

I have been thinking about the tents that the Cub Scouts had. The strings and the pegs were in just right. You could never blow them down—even I could see that, and I am just a learner. Are you very sure you want me to be like Uncle? Sometimes I wonder what is so great about him.

Anyway, I soon came to a new track. It leads to an empty place in the forest made by the woodcutter cutting down the trees there.

And guess what? There was that girl with the red hood all by herself with a picnic basket. I thought, Oh good—more chicken, I am starving. But just then, her granny came along.

And guess what? All of a suddenly, a cunning trick jumped into my head! In my mind I saw Uncle wearing the bonnet I got from Mister Twister!

I went back to Cunning College, running, running, and I said, "Listen, Uncle, I know how you can catch a nice, tasty little girl with a red hood. Why not dress up as her granny?"

Uncle said I am the stupidest pupil he has ever had. He said no way will I ever get my BAD badge now.

I am all upset.

Sniff sniff from

Little

Dear Mom and Dad,

Uncle jumped out of bed his earliest yet. He said he had thought of a brilliant way to trap that little red-hood girl—wear a bonnet and pretend to be her granny!

I said, "Uncle, I told you that. That was my idea!!"

He said, "SO WHAT?" He said if I was a really clever, cunning bad wolf, I would keep my good ideas to myself and not blab them around. He said, "SO WRITE THAT IN YOUR STUPID BOOK OF BADNESS!"

I must be a slow learner. Still, I have written it down. This is it:

RULE 8. DO NOT BLAB YOUR GOOD IDEAS.

Ho hum from

3 guesses

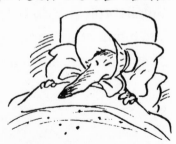

Day 30

Dear Mom and Dad,

Today I had to help Uncle get dressed up in his bonnet and granny dress and everything. He kept looking in the mirror going, "HUM, YESSS, VERY NICE, I THINK IT SUITS ME." So vain.

At last we got going to the grandma's house about lunchtime. Guess who went in and had all the fun? Yes, Uncle. He would not let me tie up the old lady or stick her in the closet. He said my job was to stay outside and give a wolf whistle if any woodcutters came along.

I hid for a while till Little Red Goodie-Hoodie came along with a basket and tip-tapped at the door. You should have heard Uncle's granny voice—it was garbage!! Even Smellybreff can do better voices. I would have run a mile if I was that girl. But she is such a simple dimple, she walked right in.

It got so boring just doing nothing. I went off and chased a few snacks in the forest, but they jumped down their holes. Boo, shame.

Then I wandered back to
Cunning College.
Big roast supper
for Uncle tonight, I 'spect.

But nothing for me.

Yours rumblytumly,

Littly

Day 31

Dear M and D,

Dear oh dear, poor old Uncle. While I was off chasing snacks, the woodcutter came along and whacked him on the bonnet with the back of his axe. Also he split him in 2 and took Little Red Goodie-Hoodie out of his tummy.

So guess what? Uncle is not feeling his best today. He said it is all my fault, and so I must suffer too.

He made me sew him up and feed him rat soup every 2 hours. I am not allowed to listen to music. And no TV, no fun at all. He kept after me about me being stupid and said I could forget the BAD badge now, *no* chance.

I have been running all over the place finding bandages to wrap Uncle's head in. He will not let me get the doctor—he says it costs too much. Also, he makes me sit by his bed and keep the flies off him. So boring!

I am a complete failure, so sorry.

Your hopeless cub,

Little

Dear Mom and Dad,

I do not know how to tell you. Something terrible has happened. I have been expelled from Cunning College.

Uncle is not fair. I nursed him and ran around for him. I even fanned him with a cabbage leaf to save from using the electric fan. But all of a suddenly, he made me write a letter to Mister Twister at Borderlands Market, like this:

MY DEAR LONG LOST CHUM,

HOW FOOLISH I WAS TO SEND YOU AWAY. RUSH TO MY AID AND I WILL REWARD YOU HANSUMLY. I AM AT DEATH'S DOOR, ALL MY NEPHEW'S FAULT.

WHEN I AM BETTER, PERHAPS WE CAN MOVE NEAR A FARM AND WORRY SHEEP TOGETHER.

HURRY. I AM ALL ALONE.
YOUR SORRY PARTNER,

BEE BEE WOLF

When I finished writing, Uncle said,
"GRRRR! NOW YOU CAN BLINKING
BLUNKING WELL BUZZ OFF. I AM TOO
POOR TO KEEP YOU."

I said, "But Uncle, I have only got 1 more
rule of Badness to learn! What about my BAD
badge?"

He said, "TOUGH LUCK. GET OUT.
YOU ARE MUCH TOO EXPENSIVE
FOR ME."

Then I made a big mistake. I said, "Ooo,
what a big miser! I bet you are rich, really."

Uncle went crackers. He jumped out of bed.
He yelled, "THAT IS A FLIPPING FLOPPING,
BIG WHOPPING LIE!!! WHO TOLD YOU I
HAVE BAGS OF GOLD STUFFED UP THE...?"

He did not finish saying stuffed up the where. He just threw cups and saucers at me and screamed, "GET OUT!!!"

Now I am all by my ownly in Frettnin Forest.

Yours chuckoutedly,

L. Wolf

Dear Mom and Dad,

Just a short note to say good-bye and sorry. I have let the family down, mostly Dad. I am a disgrace to the pack.

But do not worry, I am not coming home badgeless. I am going to hide myself deep in Frettnin Forest and hope that one day my yellow eyes will make friends with the dark and dampness.

Forgive and forget me. I shall change my name and stay far away.

Yours,

Shadow (my secret name)

Dear M and D,

Ahem. Me again. Just when I thought I was stuck being Shadow forever! Uncle has given me 1 last chance, which is...

He says he might award me my BAD badge. But only if I pass his BIG SURVIVAL TEST.

(A)   I must stay alive in Frettnin Forest with no shelter, no provisions, no nothing and

(B)   I must bring him back something big and lipsmackerous to eat from the forest.

I have got exactly 1 week to pass this test, which is a little bit too hard for me, I think, but I will give it a try.

Yours once morely,
Littly

P.S. Did I ever tell you camping out is my worst thing? Well, I think this might be even ~~worster~~ ~~wotser~~ ~~worstest~~ un~~comfortabler~~ more nasty.

Dear Mom and Dad,

Just a postcard before I curl up—no mailbox near. Still it is something to do.

Brrr! I am frozz here in the open—worse than the tent, even. I looked all day for a cave, but they have all got huge big grizzly bears inside. Also very little to eat.

Oh yes, that reminds me. I hurt myself trying a new snack today. What do they call them—hedgehogs? Talk about hot! It really burned my mouth. How was I to know you are supposed to peel them first?

Anyway, no way was that snack lipsmackerous. I do not think I will ever pass Uncle's BIG TEST.

Bbbrrr.

Your chilly boy,

Little

Dear M and D,

As you can see from the above address, I have moved. Not that it is any more comfy. I am wedged in tight like a nut in a shell. What a lousy shelter, and only a few grubs to chew.

At least the rain has stopped. About time, because my fur has gotten soggy like a rat in a gutter. It makes you feel all spooky when it stops pattering on the leaves.

I thought I heard something rustle in the bushes outside just now. Maybe Uncle has come to check me out. But he would not bother, so who is it????

Yours Ooo-erly,

Litfly

Lakeside Camp
Day 37

Dear Mom and Dad,

Oh no, trapped!!!
Now who is the simple
dimple? Me! The whistly
pack leader will put me
in a zoo tomorrow, I
know it. And I cannot
even stand my bedroom,
let alone cages!!

You know what I said about rustling? Well,
it was 2 Cub Scouts crawling through the
bushes. I thought, Funny, what are they doing
in the forest? Then I thought, Yum yum, I am
starving, and scouts look more lipsmackerous
than hedgehogs any day. I will pounce on them
silently, eat 1 and save the other for Uncle.
Then I will pass the BIG TEST, yippee.

Sad to say, my clever plan went sort of
wrong. Maybe it was my rumbling tummy, I do

not know, but all of a suddenly, 1 Cub Scout turned around and saw me lurking. He said, "Say, chum, you do not look quite well. Can we assist you in some way?"

All of a suddenly, everything went black, and when I woke up in their camp, oh no! I was zipped up to my chin in a padded bag and laid down inside a tent! Then the whistly pack leader came along saying, "Oh dear, sonny jim, you are skinny as a rake. We had better fatten you up."

Do they have fat wolf cubs in zoos? Ooo-er, maybe they are fattening me up for the cooking pot!!! Please do not tell Smells or Yeller if I end up as stew.

Yours capturedly,

Little

Dear Mom and Dad,

Arrrooooo!

Burn my last letter,
I am sooo lucky!

I am not on the menu—I
am a guest (somebody you invite to stay). That
zippy bag was not a trap, it was for sleeping!
Hmmm, cozy! They put me in it for *first aid!*

And listen to this: the pack leader says they
are going to return me to the wild as soon as I
am ready!! BUT *not before I have had lots and
lots of grub to build up my strength!*

I have just had stew, potatoes, and
bakebeans. Yum, yum, 'specially the bakebeans.
I love them. Kiss, kiss!

The boys who found me in the forest are called Dave and Sanjay. They were out playing Hide and Sneak, which is trying to creep back to the camp by the lake without your friends seeing you. Today they are going to teach it to me, and also something called Campcraft, which is great because it's true I am quite crafty, but my camping is lousy. I want to get good and surprise Uncle.

Nip Smellybreff for me and tell him it's not long now before he sees his hansum brother (this is me, and he is the ugly one going boo-hoo!!!).

Yours,

Tubby tum (get it?)

Dear Mom and Dad,

Today we did: putting up a shelter, how to stay alive if you get lost, making a shoe rack out of sticks and string, lighting a fire, and nkots (is that right?). Now I know just the right nkot for tying up grandmothers and baby brothers, so watch out, Smells! Tomorrow the pack leader says he will show us mapping and compass work and tracking. Handy for a wolf, huh? A lot better than Uncle Bigbad's lessons, if you ask me (do not tell him). Anyway, I can pass Uncle's BIG TEST easy cheesy now, I bet.

And guess what? If you join the Cub Scouts properly, you can get *lots* of badges!! But there is 1 problem, because Dave says you have to make a Cub Scout promise. So I am out of luck, because how can you be BAD and make a promise? It is too goody-goody.

Probably I shall stay here 1 more day and then go back to the forest. This is my plan: set up a best-ever camp and wait for Uncle to come and be impressed. My only small problem is finding something big and lipsmackerous to eat, but maybe something will turn up.

Then I can pass my BIG TEST, finish properly at Cunning College, get my BAD badge, and you can all be proud of me. Tell Yeller to get ready, because we are going to have a wicked time when I get home! And he will say, "Hello, Little Wolf. My, you are just like your Uncle, only badder."

Arrroooo!

~~thanks~~ ~~thanks~~

Littly

P.S. Sanjay says there is a "K" in nots, which sounds silly, but I have written one in case.

Dear Mom and Dad,

Lots to tell you. It's a good thing I like writing. Guess what, the pack leader is an Akela, same as Dad!!

Cub Scouts are great! Did you know you can earn *lots* of badges if you join? Akela said if I stayed, I could study for Camper, Explorer, Navigator, Book Reader, etc. They even have one called Animal Lover. I said, "Oh arrroooo, I am an Animal Lover, I love rabbit rolls." But Akela said that Animal Lover is not an eating badge. Oh well. Too bad.

I am really good at putting up tents now, and Hide and Sneak, and telling stories around the campfire. Today I told all about Uncle and Cunning College and the 9 Rules of Badness, and how important it is for me to get my BAD badge.

Everybody asked me what are the 9 Rules

of Badness. I said, "Sorry, I only know 8. Will they do?" And they said, "Yes, tell us." So I said,

"1. Huff and puff a lot.
2. Say lots of rude words.
3. Fib your head off.
4. Blow everybody down.
5. If it squeaks, eat it.
6. Do your dirtiest every day.
7. Do charming.
8. Do not blab your good ideas."

Dave said, "That is interesting, because the Cub Scout rules are just the opposite, and they are:

1. Do your best.
2. Think of others.
3. Do good deeds."

I said, "Har, har, good joke, Dave!" Then Akela said, "So, sonny jim, was that big, bad fellow who tried to blow our tents down the one who taught you all those nasty rules?"

So I said, "Yes, that was Uncle Bigbad."

So Akela said, "Well, I am sorry, sonny jim, but I think your uncle should not be a teacher. He should be locked away. He is a cruel, savage brute."

I said, "Gosh, thanks a lot, Akela. Uncle would be so happy to hear you say those kind words!"

Yours newsily,

L.

Dear Mom and Dad,

Today is my best day so far since I started having adventures. Guess what? I have made HISTORY!

This is what happened. I was feeling a bit sad and sorry because today was my last day with the Cub Scouts. I was in my tent packing my knapsack in the Cub Scout way (without pointy things sticking in your back). Then Sanjay came to get me.

The Cub Scouts all made a circle and I stood in the middle. Then Akela said, "Just before you go, sonny jim, we want you to take 1 or 2 things to remember us by." He said, "You have made the last few days very special for Lakeside Camp, because you are the first real wolf cub we have met. We are proud to be part of your Great Adventure, and thus and therefore, we would like to make a

presentation. So here is your special CUB
SCOUT ADVENTURE AWARD with certificate
and badge."

Can you beleeeeeve it, a BADGE! At last!!!
Plus they gave me lots of provisions, including
chocklit bars, spaghetti noodles, and 3
WHACKING big cans of bakebeans (canteen
size), because they are my favorite.

Arrroooooooooo!

from The Adventurer

Dear Mom and Dad,

I am deep in the forest where it is so dark and scary you would not beleeeeeve! Even the bats wear glasses (only kidding). But I am not scared 1 bit!

Have made this excellent shelter out of sticks and leaves (a bivouac if you want to know the proper cub scout word, hem, hem). Also I have a fire going with 1 match (stones all around to keep it from spreading—very important).

I am so warm and cozy. It is the best! And guess what I have cooked? Alphabetti spaghetti—it comes in cans. I will bring you some and show you how to open them. There you are, I have spelled

SMELLYBREFF in spaghetti and stuck it on the page for him. Good, hm?

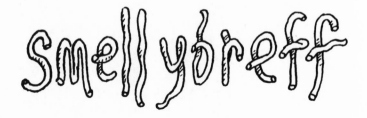

I am just waiting till midnight so that I can creep back to Cunning College and surprise Uncle. Because I have passed my BIG TEST. I am still alive after 1 week, and I have some lipsmackerous stuff for him to eat!

Yours campcraftily,

Little

Dear Mom and Dad,

Big shock!! Arrived back at Cunning College and found Uncle all tied up with rope and skinnier than ever! Cunning College was a mess—desks and furniture tipped over, trash all over. He said, "GRRRR! UNTIE ME, SWIFTLY, SWIFTLY! WHERE HAVE YOU BEEN?"

I said, "Having an adventure. Where is Mister Twister?"

He said, "HE ATTACKED ME! HE TIED ME UP! HE WAS TRYING TO FIND MY MONEY BAGS, AND NOW HE HAS WRECKED MY SCHOOL. THE BLINKING BLUNKER!"

I said, "What money bags, Uncle? I thought you were poor."

He said, "GRRRR! SILENCE, SQUIRT! CLEAN UP THIS PLACE AND GET ME SOMETHING TO EAT! I MUST LIE DOWN ON THE COUCH."

I said, "OK, I will tidy up and I will give you something lipsmackerous to eat. So now that I have passed the BIG TEST, will you give me a BAD badge after?"

Uncle said, "WHAT A MAGNIFICENT LITTLE PUPIL YOU ARE. OF COURSE YOU SHALL HAVE A BAD BADGE! BUT FOOD FIRST, BADGE AFTERWARDS."

So exciting! Must stop now because lots of work to be done.

Yours with a big

Little

Day 44

Dear Mom and Dad,

What a big cheater Uncle is! Now I am all down and dumpy again!

I cleaned up the whole college, picked up, swept up, scrubbed up, mopped up, and put away—phew! Then Uncle just gobbled up all my chocklit bars and wolfed down the rest of my spaghetti noodles. He is such a greedy-guts he did not bother to cook them or take the chocklit out of their wrappers. Then he had a long long zizz on the couch.

When Uncle woke up this morning, he said he was starving again. He thumped me with the blackboard eraser and made me cook him breakfast. I said, "But I passed my test! I lived in the forest by myself and I stayed alive. Plus I gave you something big and lipsmackerous yesterday. So give me my BAD badge and let me go!"

He said, "OH, CERTAINLY, CERTAINLY, CROSS MY HEART, STRAIGHT AFTER BREAKFAST, YOU CAN TRUST ME!"

I am down and dumpy because now I will have to cook him some of my special bakebeans, and I was saving them—1 for me, 1 for you and Smells, and 1 for Yeller.

More later on. 3 boos for Uncle.

Little

Day 44 part 2
(after breakfast)

Dear Mom and Dad,

This is kind of sad, but no presents for anybody. Sorry.

After I lit the fire, I put on the great big pot and filled it right up to the brim with my canteen-size can of bakebeans. When the beans were nice and hot, Uncle went all dribbly, and he said, "GET A BIG, BIG SPOON! FEED ME, FEED ME, SWIFTLY, SWIFTLY!"

I said, "Careful, Uncle. Bakebeans are yummy, but don't eat them too fast. Look at what the label says. Beware of the jumping beanbangs!"

But he would not look, and he would not listen. He got huffy and puffy and he threw the spoon into the corner. He yelled, "TOO SMALL! GET THE LADLE AND FEED ME, FEED ME, SWIFTLY, SWIFTLY!" So I did. He swallowed the whole pot of beans in 35 secs. Then he licked his lips, and his voice went all weak, and he said, "What about 1 more can?"

So the number 2 can that I was saving for Yeller went into the pot, canteen size again. When the bakebeans were hot, I fed them to Uncle with the ladle. Talk about a quick eater— it was like stoking the fire. Uncle said (weak voice), "Just 1 more tiny can?"

I said, "But they are my treat for my mom and dad and Smellybreff. I am saving them. I want to take them home with my BAD badge so they can be proud of me. Besides, remember the label. Beware of the jumping beanbangs!"

But he said, "GRRRR, WHO CARES ABOUT BLUNKING BLASTED BEANBANGS! GET THE COAL SHOVEL AND FEED ME, SWIFTLY, SWIFTLY!!!"

So the number 3 can that I was saving for you and Smells went into the pot—the biggest can of bakebeans you can get.

Uncle opened his mouth as wide as wide could be, and I shoveled in all the bakebeans with the coal shovel, swiftly, swiftly.

Then he smacked his horrible lips, and he rolled his horrible eyes, and he said, "NOT ENOUGH! I MUST HAVE MORE! DASH BACK TO LAKESIDE CAMP AND GET MORE BAKEBEANS, SWIFTLY, SWIFTLY!"

I said, "But Uncle, my BAD badge! You promised!"

He said, "HAR, HAR, YOU SAD, SMALL CUB! IT IS TIME I TOLD YOU RULE NUMBER 9. AND RULE NUMBER 9 IS...

NEVER TRUST A BIG BAD WOLF!"

I wish I had thought of that before.

Yours badgelessly,

Litfly

Day 45

Dear Mother and Father,

Um, what can I say? Uncle had a slight accident last night.

So I shall be quite busy burying him, etc.

Please excuse my short note.

Love,

Little

Dear Mom and Dad,

Phew, what a tiring day yesterday! Soon after the accident, Akela and the Cub Scouts came. They helped me look for Uncle. We searched all morning, but the only things we found were his whiskers and his bonnet. So it did not take long digging a grave—very small. But it took ages carving a nice message on his gravestone. Akela said it is quite good rhyming, and true—what do you think?

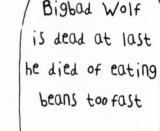

Bigbad Wolf is dead at last he died of eating beans too fast

This afternoon I found Uncle's gold BAD badge—it was hanging from the rafters.

More tomorrow.

Yours wornly,

Little

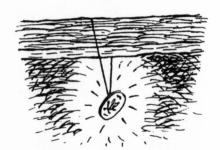

Day 47

Dear Mom and Dad,

I forgot to tell you how Uncle died. Sorry, but I was a bit busy.

It was a suddenly thing. Because after Uncle gobbled all the bakebeans, suddenly there was this great big loud noise in the night. It made me jump. I thought, Oh no, Uncle is riding his motorbike around the furniture. But no, it was not a motorbike—it was just him jumping around holding his tummy, going POP-POP-POP, KERBANG! POP-POP-POP, KERBANG!!!

I said, "Oh no, Uncle, you have got the jumping beanbangs from gobbling all those beans with the shovel! Best to stay in bed and open the window. But please, Uncle, whatever you do, do not go near the fire."

But he would not listen. He went mad. He said, "GET ME A LOG TO THUMP YOUR HEAD!" And his great big eyes were rolling, and his great big teeth were shining, and his great big *kerbangs!* were kerbanging.

I said, "Please keep away from the fire, Uncle!"

He said, "YOU CAN'T TRICK ME WITH YOUR PLEASES AND YOUR GOODY-GOODY WAYS," and he chased me around. Then he said his last words—he said,

"I'LL—*BOOM*—I'LL—*BANG*—I'LL BASH YOU FOR THIS!!! YOU—*BOOM*—YOU— *BANG*—YOU BAD LITTLE WOLF!!!"

Those were his last words, because then he bent down by the fire to pick up a log to thump me with, and

He exploded. Shame, huh? (In a way.) That is when the chimney fell over. It is lying in the garden now.

Yours sorry about not mentioning it beforely,

L.

Dear Mr. and Mrs. Moneybags and
Baby Posh,

Aha, tricked you! You thought this letter
was for somebody else, I bet! But no, you ARE
posh and moneybags now. Because guess
what? Uncle was telling big fat fibs about being
poor!! (Rule 3)

I was in the garden just now, feeling like
playing around for a while. The chimney was
lying among the flowers. So I thought, I
know—I will just have a quick game of
chimney sweeps. I like getting sooty. And I
crawled in. It was very funny and squeezy. But
the soot was so tickly, it made my nose tickle.
So I went, *Ah-hah-hah-TishINKLE!*

And do you know what the *TishINKLE*

was? It was GOLD!!! BAGS AND BAGS OF IT!!! So THAT is where Uncle had stuffed it. Up the chimney!!!

Now we are RICH.

Here I have drawn me with Uncle's gold and his big, gold BAD badge on my chest. I have awarded it to myself.

Yours deservingly,

L. B. Wolf (B for BAD, get it?)

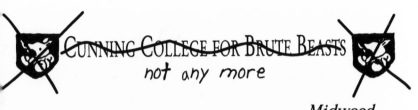

Midwood
Beastshire

Day 49

Dear Mom and Dad,

Do not worry. I will be home soon. I am
nearly ready, but not quite.

I s'pose you will say boo-hoo, what is up?
What is keeping our boy? He is rich, we are
proud of him, he knows the 9 Rules of Badness,
and he has got a gold BAD badge. Plus he hates
being away from home—it is his worst thing.
So whyo whyo Y does he not zoom back to his
nice smelly old den?

Answer—ADVENTURES. I love them, yum,
yum, kiss, kiss!! They are my best thing now. I
want lots more. BUT (big but) I do not like:

127

1. going around and around in circles getting lost

2. rain, ants, etc. down my neck

3. falling down tents

4. problems chasing snacks, etc.

5. big fibbers tricking me and being nasty to me.

So I am joining the Cub Scouts properly. Yes, I have decided to do the promise and everything. Akela is going to bring Dave and Sanjay and the rest of the Cub Scouts to camp on the college lawn. Tomorrow they are going to help me study for my Navigator badge and my Explorer badge.

Then I shall be able to find my way home, and no mistakes!

See you soonly,

L.B.W.

ADVENTURE ACADEMY

Day 50

Dear Mom and Dad,

I have changed my mind—I am not coming back home.

BUT do not howl sadly, because I am having such a good time doing my Navigator and Explorer badges. Plus, now I have decided something. I do not wish to be like Uncle Bigbad. He was really Uncle Bigsad (get it?) because he had no friends. He was all huff and puff and hot air, so it's not surprising he went out with a bang, is it?

When I grow up I want to be ME, not just some big old, horrible wolf that nobody trusts.

So guess what? I have decided to use some of the bags of money to start a new college in Frettnin Forest. And it will be called

Smellybreff and Yeller must come here right away. They can be teachers with me, and it will be the most fun school in the world. Ever!!

Also I have made the cellar nice and smelly. That means you can come and be cozy ever after!! So

(Arrroooooooo...)

From

Little Bad Wolf

P.S. I am sending you 1 bag of money. Buy Smells some fake blood, some itchy powder, a whoopy cushion, and get a pretend arrow-through-the-head for Yeller. From now on, the tricks are on me!!!!!

DA DAA

THE END